Alan Marks

The
Thief's
Daughter

Farrar Straus Giroux
New York

Chapter One

There was a girl called Magpie who lived with her mother and father in a cottage on a hillside. A windy hillside away from the town.

Although Magpie knew many stories about kingdoms and castles and harvests of gold, her family lived on a poor scrap of land. "Land that would not yield a sigh," as Magpie's mother often said.

They kept a goat, because there was not
enough grass to feed a cow. And wheat had
more dignity than to grow on this land. But
cabbage grew in plenty, and enough chickweed
to feed a few hens.

Magpie helped to pick the summer fruits and
store fuel for the winter. Mother bought flour
for bread by selling eggs or jam.

This had always been the way for Magpie,
and she was happy. But some things made her
wonder.

It was on the long winter evenings that Father told stories beside the fire in the cottage. He told of banquets, weddings, and pageants of splendor; great books bound in leather; distant voyages and strange discoveries. All the riches and mysteries of the world displayed in the courts of kings. Then the half-lit cottage might have been a great hall; the shadows that moved with the firelight were lords and ladies dancing to minstrel players.

When the wonderful stories were ended,
Magpie would hug her father and tease him for
his fanciful ideas. Turning to her mother, she'd
cry, "Imagine such things . . ." And sometimes,
looking at her mother's face, it seemed to
Magpie that Mother believed too much.
That she took Father's stories to heart.

There was another thing that worried
Magpie. Her father was a good man. But the
people around said he was a bad lot. They called
Magpie "the thief's daughter." For no good
reason. There were days when Father looked
cross and old beyond his years, when he hardly
seemed to lift his gaze from the ground. But
Magpie knew his kindness and honesty.

9

When she asked him why the people thought
he was bad, he would just say, "People believe
what they will, Pie. Sometimes things get
twisted and there's nothing short of a miracle
will make them straight."

Chapter Two

Fair weather or foul, Father worked the land. Magpie had heard it said that a man could be "as honest as the day is long." If this was so, then there could never be a man more honest than her father. He worked from cock crow till the owls hooted at the moon.

When there was no more he could do, when
you might break your back to gain a patch of
grass, Magpie would walk the bridlepaths and
roads with her father toward the town. She
skipped and ran to match his stride, chattering
all the while, pointing out clouds and birds.

He rarely spoke, or sometimes just smiled,
and never took his eyes off the ground. He
would stoop to pick up the merest thing that
glittered amid the leaf-mold and earth.

Magpie often wondered what he hoped to find. Once he found a penny, but left it on the road.

Magpie would have kept that penny. "The next man who comes along this way will find and keep it," she'd said.

"The next man who comes along this way might have dropped it," he'd replied. "I don't know who dropped it, Pie, but it isn't mine and it isn't yours. I'll know what's mine when I find it."

Sometimes he kept worthless things he found
—like a shell or a broken shoe buckle dropped
by a traveler. He said it might bring him luck.
Magpie couldn't see that
he was ever very lucky,
but he kept on looking.
Mother always said he
was looking for the past.

On clear, blue mornings, Magpie would stand on the hill behind the cottage. From there, she could see all the land between the cottage and the town. The roads she so often walked with her father looked distant and magical. The fields and woodlands held such promise. She thought she knew why her father kept looking.

Chapter Three

On one such clear morning, Magpie heard her father calling up the hill. "Magpie! Pie! I want you to go on an errand."

This usually meant going into the town. Magpie's heart sank a little. The town's people were cruel and suspicious, especially of "the thief's daughter."

"It won't take long, Pie," said Father. "Just take these eggs for Mother and see what you can get for them."

Magpie knew the road to town well. She
knew every gate and stile, each stepping-stone in
the river, and all the broken tunnels of shadow
beneath the tall trees. There was nothing
unfamiliar or disturbing about that walk into
town. This time, though, things went
differently.

When she reached the milestone that was
halfway between her home and the town,
Magpie liked to turn to look at her cottage on
the hill. This time, as she was about to turn, she
saw, just for a moment, a tall, noble lady
waiting in the road ahead.

18

Magpie stiffened a little and made ready to say, "Good day, my lady," as she'd been taught.

But as she walked on, there was no lady at all —sunlight and shadow, a rush of wind—but no lady.

"Well, that's odd," she thought. "I must have been dreaming." She peered between the trees on the roadside, and looked up and down the road. Puzzled, she scratched her head and stared blankly at the ground.

"Anyway, there was no carriage," she thought. "Such a lady would ride in a carriage."

Then she saw a key, glinting, golden in the sunlight.

At first, Magpie thought it was a penny and quickly bent to pick it up. From the moment she held the key, she knew it was special. How could something so small be so heavy? She closed her hand around the key, and still it seemed to shine. It was so beautiful, so intricately cut. It would open something very precious.

21

"Whoever lost this key will be very sorry," Magpie thought. "Finders keepers, losers weepers," she said out loud. Then she thought of what her father would say: "I don't know who dropped it, but it is not mine to keep."

Magpie decided to show the key to the people in town, to find its owner.

Chapter Four

It was market day in the town. The townspeople squabbled like birds around the stalls in the market square. There were so many people. Anyone might claim the key, but only the true owner would have the lock.

Magpie stared into the crowd, wondering if she could *see* honesty. Everyone looked so fine. Magpie gripped the golden key tightly, remembering what her mother said about fine feathers not making fine birds.

"An honest man might go about in rags," she thought.

There happened to be a match-seller nearby. He was the most ragged man Magpie had ever seen. Who was to say he was not the most honest?

Magpie looked up at the match-seller and said, "Please, sir, I found this key."

The match-seller looked down at the golden key shining in Magpie's hand. He had never seen anything so beautiful. He was speechless.

Before he could utter a word, an old woman in the crowd pointed to Magpie and called, "Look out! It's the thief's daughter."

Magpie had been taught always to be polite. She fought back angry tears. She bit her lip and bravely repeated, "Please, I found this key." Now everyone was looking at her.

"Such a beautiful key," the match-seller finally gasped.

"What's he saying?" called another in the crowd.

"The thief's daughter says she's found a key," said the old woman.

"Stole it, more like," came the voice from the crowd.

All the crowd moved toward little Magpie. She wished now she had not been honest. It would have been better to have left the key on the road, or to have taken it home. Magpie thought again of her father and knew what she had done was right. But the crowd thought she was a thief.

The old woman moved even closer. In her fright, Magpie dropped the key and her mother's eggs.

"I'll take that key you stole!" snapped the old woman, and would have snatched it if a clear voice had not spoken above the rabble: "That key belongs to my household."

Everyone turned to see who spoke. Magpie recognized the noblewoman she had seen on the road. She seemed to be taller than anyone in the crowd.

Her voice, though not loud, rang as clear as a distant bell. She spoke again, "It was lost many years ago from my family. The child has done me a great service by finding and returning this key. There are bigger thieves here than a magpie."

Chapter Five

The voices in the crowd fell silent.

Magpie wondered how the lady knew her name, but she dared not breathe. She looked down at the basket of eggs, broken on the cobblestones, and at the bright key nearby. She wondered which was the more precious: a key with no lock to open, or broken eggs that would buy no flour.

From a far corner of the market, the traders' cries began once more. "Who will buy my rosy red apples? Who will buy . . . ?"

"And who will buy my broken eggs?"
thought Magpie.

Soon the crowd had moved away.

Magpie knelt to see what eggs could be saved.
She thought she'd leave the key where it was.

"*Finders keepers* you said, Magpie." The lady
had knelt down with her. "You'd better keep
the key."

"I don't want it," said Magpie, hardly daring to look at the lady's face. "It's brought nothing but sorrow."

By this time Magpie really wanted nothing to do with golden keys, or with grand ladies that came and went with the wind. She wished her father had been there. He knew what to keep and what to leave behind.

The lady was standing now. Magpie didn't like the way she moved so quickly and without making any noise.

The lady said, "On the day you were born, there was never a happier man than your father. On that day, he also lost a great deal. He called you Magpie for sorrow and for joy."

Magpie trembled a little. "What do you know about my father? How do you know my name?"

"Take the key to your father," said the lady. "Tell him he always had the trust of his Queen."

"Queen!" cried Magpie. She looked down again at the golden key and then turned to look at the lady, but once more she had gone.

"What an errand this is turning out to be," Magpie said to herself.

Chapter Six

Magpie gripped the key in her hand. She was on the road back home. The eggs hadn't brought a penny, and she feared that her father would be angry with her. First for dropping the eggs and then for keeping the key.

She had a very uneasy feeling about that noble-woman. Was she really a queen, and how did she know about Father? He was only a poor farmer. He didn't have anything to do with queens.

When she reached the halfway milestone, Magpie thought to look back on the road. But then she thought better of it. She could make out her mother and father working on the land near the cottage. She ran all the rest of the way home, without looking back once.

When Magpie's father saw the key, he was not angry at all. He looked at her in wonder. In a very soft voice, he asked, "Where did you find this?"

"On the road," said Magpie. "Just past the milestone."

"Oh, Pie, I've searched that road a thousand times . . ." began Father.

He went into the cottage and came back with a small wooden box. The box was very old and quite plain, but the lock was inlaid with gold as intricately cut as the key. Magpie was sure she had not seen the box before. She would have remembered something that beautiful.

Father fitted the key into the lock and turned it once, twice, three times for luck. The lid of the box clicked open.

"But, Father, what does this mean?" asked Magpie.

"Long ago, Pie, before you were born . . ." Father began.

"Is this another of your stories?" said Magpie.

"It's a true story," said Father. "All the stories are true. Before you were born, I held high office in the royal household. The Office of the Keys, a trustworthy post. The court was open to whoever held those keys. I never betrayed that trust.

"By chance, though, on the day you were born, I lost the King's keys on the road. I was too happy or too foolish to take care. I searched the roads all the rest of that day but did not find even one of those keys. Whoever did find them stole a great deal from the King. When I returned to the court that night, I was thought to be the thief. I could say nothing to prove that that was untrue. The King was blind with rage. I was thrown out of office, and might have been executed but for the Queen."

"The Queen!" gasped Magpie.

"The Queen pleaded for my life," continued Father. "She gave me this box as a symbol of her trust. When the Queen died, I thought my heart would break."

"But she can't be dead," insisted Magpie. "I spoke to her. She said to tell you that you always had her trust—and then she disappeared!"

Magpie shivered, and
Father's hands trembled
as he held the box.

"The good Queen must be in heaven,"
whispered Mother, "but she came back to show
you the key."

Still trembling, Father opened the box. Inside the lid, written in gold, it said:

TO BREAK THE LOCK WOULD
BREAK MY TRUST
AN HONEST MAN WILL HAVE
THE KEY

The box held papers bearing the seal of the royal household. Father read them carefully.

"These deeds belong to whoever holds this golden key," he said. "They give us land, good land."

"Is it half a kingdom?" cried Magpie.

Father looked at her and smiled, and he seemed to grow taller. "No," he said. "It's enough land for an honest man to make a good living."

Magpie turned to look back down the hill to the milestone. Just for a moment, she thought she saw a glint of gold.